CW01073126

Published in the United Kingdom by
ElzDan Publications, 27 Glamis Road,
Dundee, Scotland. DD2 1TS.

A CIP record of this book is available from the British Library.

First printed March 2019.

ISBN 978-0-9933194-2-6

Design by Stuart Cameron @ design100.

Illustrations by Keith Walker.

For copies of the book, e-mail:
watson.glamis@blueyonder.co.uk

Intro

From the first day I set foot in Dundee the beauty of its river caught my breath and my imagination. But it's not just Dundee's river, the Tay's beauty stretches through centuries of history and mystery, through glens where the river and its tributaries flow, dwarfed by mountains and majestic surrounds of history, legend, peoples and fable.

Picts and Celts, Romans and Scots voyaged the river's banks and braes on a Tardis of time. The language of many tongues echoed through the squalls of its grieving clouds and the panoramas of its sunglow. The tongues of our ancestors, Latin, Brythonic, Gaelic, Auld Scots, and our varied vernaculars of universal English.

The poem tries to interweave, with little sense of order in its timescape and language, the histories and mysteries, tragedies and triumphs of our great river.

It is perhaps less than perfect that one of the most abiding images of the Tay should be in the oft-quoted rhymes of William McGonagal.

I came by chance on a much more rewarding representation of the Tay, from its source high on Ben Lui to Stanley on the skirts of Perth. A wonderful book, 'The Highland Tay', beautifully portrays the many aspects of its flora and fauna and centuries of lives lived.

It was written by a 19th century minister called Hugh Macmillan. Born in Aberfeldy, he began his ministry at the Free Church in Breadalbane.
The book which, throughout, reveals his great love of the river, provided the inspiration and wealth of knowledge for this poem. Without it, it could never have been written.

Harrison Watson.

The Poem

The Histories and Mysteries of The Highland Tay

Tatha stairts up wi' a riddle,
Like a blin' bow on a fiddle,
As it jigs a raggit reel alang the pass.
Frae Ben Laoigh's upper corrie,
Twistin like a huntit quarry,
Oft retreating in some happit neuk o' grass.

And the infant stream then tosses,
Throu the tufted, mountain mosses,
Which are kin to its translucent, chartreuse brose.
Then throu rushing rocks of sunshine,
Exulting wildly in that vert wine,
Where its Fillan waters kittle Dalree's toes.

Through the lament o' the King's Field,
Where Macdougall made The Bruce yield,
And in gore the precious Gem of Lorne was stolen.
Hear the wail of tragic waters,
Hurl the echoed Doran's daughters
To seek sanctuary where streams of tears are swollen.

• **Corrie:** *a hollow between hills*
• **Happit:** *covering, concealing*
• **Kittle:** *tickle*
• **Flichtie:** *fickle*

4

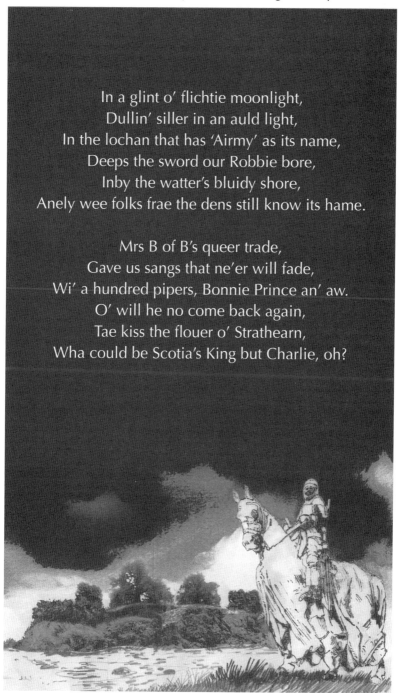

In a glint o' flichtie moonlight,
Dullin' siller in an auld light,
In the lochan that has 'Airmy' as its name,
Deeps the sword our Robbie bore,
Inby the watter's bluidy shore,
Anely wee folks frae the dens still know its hame.

Mrs B of B's queer trade,
Gave us sangs that ne'er will fade,
Wi' a hundred pipers, Bonnie Prince an' aw.
O' will he no come back again,
Tae kiss the flouer o' Strathearn,
Wha could be Scotia's King but Charlie, oh?

Then to Tyndrum, less remote,
Where the leaded mines yinst smote
Wearied pickmen's lives aneath a thackit sky.
Tae St Fillan's blessed well,
Which could dafties' dwaums dispel,
And deluge their wildert fancies, tossed and tied.

Throu Strathfillan, Crianlarich,
Past the raggle o' Glenfalloch,
To Loch Dochart in the cradle o' Ben More,
Where the lissom Arctic willows
And dwarf birches kissed the pillows
Of saxifrage mossed bricht doon on the shore.

Daurk the rocks that hang and dim,
Yon Echo Cave on Dochart's rim,
Haven for a Clan the mists held naur.
Echoes whisper aye the words,
Screeded by the Soothern bard,
'Wild eagles lord above, Red Rob belaw.'

Sic a sicht o' hazel swamps,
Where the wild boars' runtin' romps
Hounded bears and wolves tae pack and yowl.
And the knolls and crags on high
Reive the river for the sky,
As Macgregor's castle shidders in the bowl.

Look, the marshy meadow's riddle,
Tries the current's rocky idyll,
Where the pearl was found that kisst The Bruce's crown.
And the spectre o' the glen,
Haunts the oorie wraiths of men,
Drifting opaline upon the lupine sound.

At Killin the rapids smile,
Freithin roon Garbhinish Isle.
Yon Stobinian, Ben More's flaxen twin,
Where the Celtic moon at night
Weaves its spells o' hoary light,
As sepulchral fairies dance aroon' its rim.

- **Thackit:** *thatched*   - **Runtin:** *wild*
- **Dwaums:** *dreams*   - **Reive:** *steal*
- **Wildert:** *bewildered*   - **Oorie:** *eerie*
- **Naur:** *near, close*   - **Freithin:** *frothing*
- **Screeded:** *written*

By the graves beside the river,
Fingal's hillheid tomb still shivers,
As it glimps the yellae island o' the banes,
There MacNab ghaists sunken lie,
Neath the mirk that is the sky,
And their fykie spirits issue frae the stanes.

Ha'penny fields are weel spent whaur,
The Drovers Roads are forhoued aw,
Nae Celtic oxen's affspring hirdin throu.
Lanesome scots pines steer the way,
Soor o' nicht or dour o' day,
For drover men sae birsie and sae prood.

Oats and whiskey war their fare,
Puddins black wi' blood tae share,
Swuirds and dirks forfend the reiver raids.
Past some oorie coffin stone,
Paidlin floods and kempin storm,
Ontae their tryst, tapsmen, ponies and plaids.

- **Glimps:** *sights.*
- **Banes:** *bones.*
- **Mirk:** *gloom.*
- **Fykie:** *restless.*
- **Forhoued:** *forsaken.*
- **Soor:** *cold and wet.*

- **Birsie:** *dogged.*
- **Forfend:** *defend.*
- **Oorie:** *gloomy.*
- **Kempin:** *braving.*
- **Tapsmen:** *head drovers.*

Finlanrig castle, Loch Tay's gaird,
Black Duncan's cheen-pits never spared
Moot Hill's sair victims frae the Hanging Tree.
The magic stane that never dries,
Yinst healt wee weans' whoopin cries,
Whiles fowerteen knichtheids keek but never see.

To the East, they lang green flouers
Are the fingers o' Ben Lawers,
As its storm-scaurred summit glowers on Loch Tay,
Where the garnet crystal bed
Straiks the salmon silver red,
And the Rock of Holes is altar to the day.

- **Cheen:** chain
- **Knicht:** knight
- **Lowp:** leap
- **Waesome:** sorrowful
- **Clachan:** village
- **Sabbin:** weeping
- **Claucht:** clawed

See the rare forget-me-not
Coronet the lanesome spot,
As its turquoise tops the mounts of Breadalbane,
Where the rampant alpine hare
Lowps a lowp and stares a stare,
At the sair croak o' a ptarmigan's refrain.

On the knolls, bereft and lanely,
By the weeping streams of faimily,
Grim ruins o' despair and desolation.
Waesome crofts, auld clachans sabbin,
Clearances o' reivin', grabbin',
Ill jaws of sheep claucht ploumen frae the nation.

The tarn o' Loch-na-cat unseen,
Whaur the burn linns mist and screen,
Macgregors' cave is happit frae the skies.
A bloodhoond, suckled by their ain,
Dourly socht his scent in vain,
Gin an arrow blindit its Italian eyes.

At the clach o' Fortingal,
The Gallar Plague's dreid pall
Is myndit by a cairn they call The Dead.
On Craig Dianaig's sauftie hill,
St Eonan's staff did still
Glenlyon's dreid the pestilence would spread.

The Fort of Strangers, cauld and smirt,
Moated site withert in dirt,
Cradelt a roman wraith, cruel-crossed for pain.
Hauf-Druid bairn, born to duim
The saviour son intae death's womb,
While the yew of ages shiddert in God's rain.

• **Linns:** *cascades.*
• **Happit:** *hidden.*
• **Socht:** *searched.*
• **Clach:** *small town.*
• **Myndit:** *remembered.*

• **Sauftie:** *safety.*
• **Dreid:** *dread.*
• **Smirt:** *drizzled.*
• **Duim:** *doom.*

Kenmore, on the watter born,
Rustic dwellings yinst adorned,
Enfaulded by the woods o' Drummond Hill.
And in Taymouth Castle Square,
At the Inn still standing there,
The Bard's inspired eyes wi' wonder filled.

The infant Tay meandering douce,
Tae maist luesomely seduce
The gentle braes that curve wi' careless taste.
In a wink o' nuintide beam,
Gracefu' arches stride the stream,
The Makar wi' ayebidin verses graced.

*The arches striding o'er the new born stream
The Village glittering in the noontide beam.*

And sometimes in the Square,
The Holy Women's Fair
Wad bless the Sisters o' the Isle of Tay,
Whose castle, once sublime,
Yieldit, in daurker times,
Tae Cromwell's monk who blessed in Satan's way!

On Drummond's Rock of Shouting,
A bleak spurtle on the mountain,
Your yauls tae Dun Mac Tual will carry faur,
Where wild warriors and criers
Lit the bleizin cross o' fires,
Harbinging the monstrous cull of war.

Sycamore and oaks and birches
Form an avenue that stretches
To Aberfeldy's golden sheaves of caution.
And the stones at Fields of Mary
Mark a pagan sanctuary,
Where the silent sun sips Ruskin's 'pools of pausing'.

• **Luesomely:** *lovingly.*
• **Spurtle:** *spoon.*
• **Yaul:** *shout.*

Roond the river's lissom bend,
In a quest that has no end,
A flame-haired lassie rakes her dreams, days aw,
For a treasure that's concealed,
Where the Fort of Dun reveals
The slackie loch that hides itself awa.

On a stream that rins faur East,
Andrea Ferrara's smiddie cast
The iron blades that yield nae second wound.
On Wade's military route,
Charlie's bra' young lads set foot,
And their ghaists lament ill winds o' spectral soond.

'Mid the birks on Tulloch Heights,
Moness water fa's as bright
As the blessed haar on Celtic Avalon.
Cascade upon cascade,
In the feathered, woodland shade,
Chase waves o' light on silverin' beams of morn.

- **Rake:** *to search for.*
- **Slackie** – *a hollow between hills.*
- **Chitterin:** *shivering.*
- **Yammers:** *laments.*

Splutter splatter goes the watter,
Dreepin frae the rocks sae battered,
By the roarin linn, like thunner birlin free.
Hear the craw caw as it glowers
On yont chitterin siller showers,
Wairnin dire, o' days o' do or dee.

In the hollow of Loch Hoil,
The wicked woman's call
Still yammers through the shrood o' stygian day.
And a Hielander on high
Thraws bold shadows tae the sky,
Le Garde Noir de Les Soldats Ecossais.

In outrage foams the Tay,
Where Wade's brig betrays the day
Its beauty mocked the history o' the oor.
It welcomed Johnny Cope,
And gied Cumberland the rope
Tae snare the bloom o' snell Culloden's floer.

At Weem there's seven gates,
Whaur a stricken sister waits,
Mistraucht afore the sentry's scarlet cloak.
And a voice manes far away,
In tones of plaided grey,
'Seek me floating in Loch Glassie's phosphor smoke.'

Castle Menzies westward lies,
Where the bagpipe sings and sighs,
Of Bannockburn's triumph hear it play.
And the Red Book screeds a talk
Of the shade royal Mary walked,
Aneath the sycamore that bears her name today.

• **Mistraucht:** *distraught.*
• **Mane:** *a cry of sorrow.*
• **Screed:** *a piece of writing.*

The river bygaes Rock of Cluny,
Near the mounds that mark Grandtully,
Look! the raging Lyon roars the rapids through.
There the Plain of Appin lies,
Where the Strath's green beauty cries
Tears of violet and sweet primrose-buttered hue.

Hillside burns alive wi' trout
Leap and, sparkling, seem to shout
At the tapestries of bell-heather and broom.
And the heron-haunted tarn
Holds a mirror to the baron,
Where the Druids' hazel brambles hush and bloom.

Roses, waesome, dreich wi' tears,
Frae Ballechin's hauntit years.
Rose slew a squire, then fled frae fear o' blame.
In the rannochs, love betrayed,
And knichts' claymores vengefu' slayed.
A wild hert tamed, a spearheid its last hame.

• **Bygaes:** *passes.*
• **Waesome:** *sorrowful.*
• **Dreich:** *bleak.*
• **Rannoch:** *ferns, bracken.*
• **Berg:** *a prominent rock.*

At the Court of Logierait,
Doomed souls hadna lang tae wait,
The wee walk to Gallow Hill was in ticht hands.
Rob Roy brak the hangman's bind,
But naewhere will you find
The fate of the 'Six Hunder Prestonpans'.

On yonder moor's high lip,
The ancient berg's worship,
To West a blessing, East the Druid's blight.
Dunfallandy's sculptured stone
Haud's a Celtic tale unknown,
As it's mystic figures mote a Crescent's sight.

And from desolate Drumochter,
Slaking Atholl's vale wi' water,
The Garry's thirst for beauty is assuaged.
But the mountain lawns o' green
Sleely steal it to the scene,
Where the Pass of Killiecrankie's battle raged.

Gruesome leaves still shiver sadly,
As the aspens mourn the valley,
Where Dundee, on his dun horse, strode the Lude.
And his charge from high upby
Skeiched the Royals and Mackay,
As the Hielan' broadswords carnaged them wi' blood.

The first Orange sodger fell
At some airt called Horsemen's Well,
Ban Beg MacRon's aim was true and prood.
But the last musket of a'
Saw the Bonnie Dundee fa',
And the flag o' victory became his shrood.

Yes, the aspen leaves all shivered,
As the rush of men delivered,
Death and Bedlam for their wives' and mithers' fears.
Three thoosan' bra' lads were the losses,
For the sake of Kings and Crosses,
And the winner, Cluit the Deil, spraiched nae tears.

A hunder silver threads,
Frae a hunder hills are fed,
Ballinluig weds wild Tummel to the Tay.
And the looming Mount of Blood
Taints the air and feeds the flood
O' auld claivers of assassins and their prey.

* **Sleely:** *with guile.*
* **Skeiched:** *duped.*
* **Airt:** *place.*
* **Spraich:** *the sound of weeping.*
* **Claivers:** *gossip.*

Frae Loch Freuchie flows the Braan,
Tae the crooked brig that spans,
Near tae Inver where the music man was born.
Neil Gow's Strathspeys and Reels
Captivated Scotia's chiels,
As 'Farewell to Whisky' echoed heilan' scorn.

Fairy flames o' red and peach,
Tint autumnal ash and beech,
As the Tay through Dunkeld's vale is hewn.
Clouds o' fir, tourin the larches,
Wraith doon on the seven arches,
Whose daurk shadows circle each transparent noon.

Craig-y-Barns and Craig Vinean,
Bare and gaunt were ever seen,
Till the Duke of Atholl's canisters of seed,
Scaitered wide wi' cannons' blast,
Drilled a harvest that would last,
And wi' greens o' Spring, the steeps wi' velvet bleed.

• **Tourin:** *towering over.*
• **Lourin:** *lurking.*
• **Weel:** *a deep pool.*
• **Lin :** *rest.*

Gaunt, the lourin mountain tops,
Feed the Tay wi' gallus rocks,
As, abruptly, it eludes the distant hills.
Floods o' beauty soothe the soul,
Wi' a calmness that beholds
Weels of wonder where our dreams lin deep and still.

Yonder Hill of Dunsinane,
Tourin' on the Sidlaw range,
Hosts an auld fort spawning tales o' great Macbeth,
Where the Birnam woods walked high,
Wi' a furtive battle cry,
All hail tae the Royal tragedie of death.

But the mellow curfew bell,
Casts the auld Cathedral's spell,
Whispering in the woodlands, murmuring in the streams,
As the Tay through Birnam Pass,
Widens, breathes its Hielan' last,
As it smooths and deeps and faur tae Perth it gleams.

Septimus' twa thoosand men,
Mairched up the hill and doun again,
Their fort sae stark, high on the Gaskhill line.
Antlers o' wid rut their retreat,
Frae Graupius glory, drear defeat,
Their Pompeii pots bitter wi' tears o' wine.

On the East bank drifts Meikleour,
Wi' beech hedges lang and pure,
As the Scottish blood that soaked Culloden red.
Luesome planted by Jean Mercer,
Whose guidman Rob bereft her,
When Prince Charlie wairnt him tae the Fields of Dead.

And doonstream, the lore o' Stanley,
Whaur the Thistle Brig yinst stood by,
As wildert Norsemen creeped the river dark.
But our sleepin clansmen wakened,
By a shriek of stealth forsaken,
As the emblem o' the thistle left its mark.

- **Luesome:** *lovingly.*
- **Wairnt:** *summoned.*
- **Lee lane:** *all alone.*
- **Dirl:** *shiver with emotion.*

Noo the fiddle wi' its blin' bow
Reels its last and mutes a sad flow,
Tatha forsakes its hert, its heilan' hame.
And its sang yearns sad a pibroch,
As it pines sair for its hame loch,
And the rugged Scotia beauty left lee lane.

But alway the hert can shiver,
As its dreams caress the river,
Whaur a wild untempert splendour dirls the soul.
As its mountains kiss the sky,
As its glens still smile or sigh,
And the chimes o' grief or glory soar or toll.

The
Prose

The River Tay's gaelic name is Tatha. Its source is thought to be in a corrie, Allt Coire Laoigh, two thousand feet high on the eastern side of Ben Laoigh (Ben Lui), somewhat on the border of Perthshire and Argyll, about 25 miles from Oban.

The Tay is, at 120 miles in length, the longest river in Scotland. It has the largest discharge of any river in the UK, carrying a greater volume of water than the Thames and Severn combined.

Its long history of flooding saw severe floods in 1210 and 1648 destroy the bridges at Perth.

In the late 19th century the river would freeze hard enough for 'the roaring game' of curling to be playeds.

In its upper course the Tay takes on a number of different names, including Connonish, Fillan and Dochart.

The river, with the splendour of its beauty, caused the ancient Roman invaders to compare it to the Tiber. It has a myriad of tributaries including the Earn, Tummel, Isla, Almond and Lyon.

On its long journey to Perth It flows through Lochs Dochart, Lubhair and Tay. It becomes tidal beyond Perth and is famous for its Atlantic Salmon and freshwater pearl mussels.

Page 4

In 1306 The Battle of Dalree was fought between King Robert the Bruce and the Madougalls of Lorne. The location of the battle still bears the name of The King's Field, near Dalree.

The battle was in revenge for the murder of Red Comyn, Earl of Badenoch, nephew of the Macdougall chief and rival for the Scottish throne. He was stabbed to death by Bruce in the Dumfries Church of Greyfriars.

Overpowered by numbers in the battle, Bruce's forces retreated through a narrow pass near Loch-an-Our.

Tradition has it that, in a brave skirmish with his pursuers, Bruce lost his cloak and the jewel which fastened it – the beautiful Brooch of Lorne. The brooch is still conserved in a trust by the Macdougall family, as a memorial of the battle.

There is also a belief, passed through the memories of time, that during the pursuit, Bruce's massive sword, over six feet in length, was thrown into the waters of Lochan nan Arm ('Loch of the Army'). It may lie there to this day.

Page 5

The whole area around the Tay is musically alive with Jacobite songs and stories of Prince Charlie. A lady, largely unrecognised and forgotten, Carolina Oliphant, who became Baroness Nairne, wrote many poignant lyrics to old Scottish tunes. She described this hobby as 'Practising a queer trade'.

She was born in Gask, where her family were staunch followers of the Jacobite cause.

Written under the pen name of Mrs Bogan of Bogan or 'BB', many of her songs are still known and loved today. Ironically, because of her wish for anonymity, some may have been attributed to others, including Robert Burns.

Her songs include 'Wha'll Be King But Charlie?', 'Charlie is My Darling', 'Wi' a Hundred Pipers', 'Bonnie Charlie's Noo Awa' and 'Will Ye No Come Back Again?'.

Lady Nairne also wrote much-loved songs like 'The Rowan Tree' and 'The Auld Hoose.' And the amusingly satirical poem, 'The Laird O' Cockpen'.

In her day, Carolina Oliphant was so famed for her beauty she was known as 'The Flower of Strathearn'.

Page 6

At Tyndrum, the river is known as Fillan Water. Tyndrum's gaelic name, Taigh an Druim, translates as the 'House on the Hill'. It used to be a mining centre for lead ore and the surrounding slopes are known to have silver and gold deposits.

Tyndrum is a sanctuary for the meeting of the streams and waterfalls from Ben Doran and Ben Laoigh. And the 'music of many waters' can fill the listening air.

The renowned Holy Pool of St Fillan is associated with pagan rites such as sun worship and was considered sacred.

From ancient times the pool was thought to hold the cure for certain illnesses, especially mental. From near and far, crowds of people came, hoping to be healed. They had to bring up nine pebbles from the bed of the pool and place them on cairns on the hilltop. If their infirmity was thought to be madness, they would be tied to a rope and thrown in. The shock was professed to 'put you right'!

A piece of clothing that covered a patient's particular ailment was tied to trees or bushes to transfer the disease and complete the cure.
On a nearby flat and sacred rock, cakes were made from meal mixed with holy water from the pool. These were given, as a cure, to diseased cattle and horses.

The village of Strathfillan is named after St Fillan. His festival was observed annually on January 9th, thought to be the day that he died in 770 AD. He was the patron saint of the mentally ill and gave his blessing to the Holy Pool of his name.

Legend has it that he came from an Irish family of Gaels. Tales tell that, because he was born with a stone in his mouth, his father threw him into a lake where he was rescued by angels.

His relics were used to inspire the army of Robert the Bruce before the Battle of Bannockburn. In thanks Bruce later established St Fillan's Priory.

St Fillan lived most of his life as a hermit in a cave at Pittenweem, which means 'place of the cave'.

To the North of Loch Dochart there's an eerie cave – The Cave of Echoes. It's difficult to reach, having to be approached by swimming round protruding cliffs. An ideal place of refuge in perilous times.

It is thought Rob Roy Macgregor had a farm close by on Ben More. The cave was probably a hiding place for members of the Macgregor Clan when they were outlawed, 'altogidder abolisheed', having fallen out of favour with King James VI, who hanged their Clan Chief at Edinburgh's Mercat Cross.

So adept were they at evading the Redcoats and other enemies, the Macgregors became known as the 'Children of the Mist'.

As its name implies, an incredible echo can be heard in the cave. It seems to repeat phrases of words with great clarity. Whether William Wordsworth, in his visit to the area, actually recited in the cave, the words, 'The eagle he was lord above and Rob Roy lord below', from his famous poem, 'Rob Roy's Grave' is a matter of conjecture.

Page 7

Macgregor's Castle was on the site of a picturesque ruin on a wooded island in Loch Dochart. Stolen by the Campbells of Lochawe (and later rebuilt as Loch Dochart Castle), it was thought to be impregnable due to the deep waters of the loch. But it was retaken by the Macgregors at a time of temperatures so severe that the loch froze solid.

Advancing over the ice behind huge fascines of straw and branches, to protect them from a hail of arrows, they managed to scale the walls and subdue their foes.

For centuries The Tay was famous for freshwater pearls – 'amongst the finest in the world'. They are valued for their beauty and rarity, with a colour and lustre 'that often surpasses that of fine oriental pearls'. Characterised by a rich variety of natural tints, they have distinctive shapes which makes every stone unique.

Undisturbed, freshwater mussels can live for more than fifty years – sometimes, it has been said, to a length of several inches. Scottish pearl mussels are now a protected species, since over-exploitation seriously endangered their survival.

'A pearl of great price', one of the finest ever found, embellished the crown of King Robert the Bruce.

Page 8

One of the primitive races, living among the hills and glens of Tayside, buried their dead in cists on raised mounds. These sombre knolls were believed to be the abode of fairies. On moonlight nights they would dance on the high ridges, seeking to enchant any mortal who set eyes on them.

On a hill behind Killin a large mound is thought to be the burial place of Fingal, the ancient Scottish warrior made famous in the Ossian poems of James MacPherson. He is most commonly remembered for Staffa's celebrated Fingal's Cave.

One translation of the name Killin is 'the grave beside the river'.
The 'yellow island' is Inch Buie, the age-old burial ground of the MacNab Clan chiefs. Holed stones, on the graves are said to let the spirits of the dead escape to revisit their former lives.

Cattle, historically, were vital to the lives of highlanders, with much of the land unsuited to growing crops. Drovers would drive herds long distances along 'drovers roads' to market towns like Crieff and Falkirk.

The cattle, smaller and hardier than todays, were largely descendents of ancient Celtic oxen.

The drovers would bargain for cattle in local farms. They would build up herds of at least a hundred, then start their long, hazardous journey to their market 'trysts'. Often hundreds of them could be seen sleeping in the open with their dogs and ponies till their cattle were sold to buyers from all over Britain.

The drovers roads were sometimes marked by trees, often Scots Pines. The herds would travel about ten miles a day. They would stop to graze at farmers or inn-keepers 'ha'penny fields' at a cost of two for a penny.

Sometimes their dogs would be left to find their own way home, stopping for food at inns known to them. The innkeepers would be paid a small annual fee for this service,

The roads from Killin and Tyndrum would lead to the 'tryst' in Crieff.

Page 10

Finlanrig Castle was once the family seat of the House of Breadalbane. It guarded the pass where the River Lochay enters Loch Tay.

The most infamous and barbarous of the castle's feudal barons was Black Duncan of the Cowl. Beneath the basement of the now-ruined castle lie the dungeons where his doomed prisoners were chained to the walls, whilst Lords and Ladies would dance and feast in the splendid rooms above.

The castle was last occupied when Royal troops used it as a garrison in the Jacobite Rebellion of 1745.

Nearby, a giant sycamore was for centuries the notorious Hanging Tree. Lawbreakers, tried in the open-air court of Dunlochay, held on 'Moot Hill', were executed there.

East of Auchmore, near the Loch Tay shore, lies a moss-obscured boulder. High on its side is a natural hollow in which rain water would gather. It was called the Whooping Cough Stone. Children with this ailment would be taken here. They would climb two or three steps to reach the hollow whose miraculous waters could cure them.

Sheltered by an overhang, it was claimed that magical bowl of water would never evaporate.
The Breadalbane mausoleum, on the site of an ancient chapel to the Blessed Virgin, looks sombrely across the valley. Fourteen of the

Knights of Glenorchy, the Baronets and Earls of Breadalbane, rest here.

Into Loch Tay flow the united rivers Dochart and Lochay. Here, on the yellow siliceous sand bed, are areas of tiny, bright red garnet crystals, washed down from mountain burns. In times gone by, people used to make strops for sharpening scythes from this fine garnet sand.

The Rock of Holes beneath Ben Lawers is a peculiar rock surface called Craggantol. Its surface is pitted with cup hollows. It is possibly an ancient sun altar where primitive peoples would see the sun's eastern rising and the embryonic mountain summit in the dawn mists. From earthen pitchers they would pour water from the nearby stream into the cuplike holes, till the sun in its full power would drink them dry.

Page 11

East of Killin, above the dark velvet waters of Loch Tay, ghostly ruins of crofts and hamlets can still be seen.

In many communities in northern Scotland, the populace was driven out by landowners, during the infamous 'Highland Clearances'. This was to make way for more profitable sheep farming. Gaelic people whose forefathers had tilled the land for generations suffered compulsory eviction, often to coastal crofts and a life of subsistence.

Cottages were burned to prevent their return.

In time disease, starvation and despair led to mass migration to lowland towns or overseas to Canada, Australia and the United States – a pattern of rural depopulation and the destruction of Clan society and Gaelic culture.

One of the predictions of the famous soothsayer, 'The Lady of Lawers', was that, 'The jaw of the sheep will drive the plough from the ground'.

Page 12

A burn, running from the tarn of Ben Lawers' Loch-na-cat, issues as a veil of cascades. It conceals a cave which once gave refuge to an outlawed Macgregor. The story is that an italian bloodhound was used in the search for him. This curious breed was said to have been suckled by a Macgregor woman to focus the animal on tracking that particular Clan.

The pursuers had called off the search, but the dog remained, sniffing closer and closer to the cave. Macgregor then fired an arrow which killed him – the last hound of that dreaded breed.

At the end of the seventh century Scotland was ravaged by the Gallar Mohr, a devastating plague. In Fortingall an elderly lady, the only one left alive, buried the dead villagers in a large hollow. Later, a cairn of stones was built over the gravesite. It became known as 'The Cairn of the Dead'.

As the plague spread, the people in Glenlyon begged St Eonan, one of the early Celtic saints, for help. Standing on a hill, he struck a rock with his staff and beseeched God to hold back the pestilence. His success was so remarkable the hill was named Craig Dianaig – The Hill of Safety.

A translation of Fortingall is 'The Fort of the Strangers'. This depicts the Roman Camp built during the reign of druidic king Metallanus, who lived around the time of Jesus. It is claimed by some historians to be the birthplace of Pontius Pilate, the Governor of Judea who was responsible for the trial and subsequent crucifixion of Christ.

Pilate's father was thought to be a Roman delegate negotiating with King Metallanus. He married a local woman who produced a baby – Pontius Pilate. The child and mother were dispatched back to Rome.

The 'yew of ages' is the famous Fortingall Yew, which, though greatly damaged, still stands in the village churchyard. It is thought be around 5000 years old.

Page 13

The village of Kenmore could be said to have been water-born, grown out of Loch Tay. In the 16th century it was only a ferry station, its sole house being the ferryman's. He carried people across the Tay where it flows from the loch.

On a visit to Kenmore in 1787, Robert Burns was so impressed by the beauty of the village and its river, he composed a poem while standing on the bridge. Later he wrote lines of the poem in pencil above the fireplace in what is now called 'The Poet's Bar' in the Kenmore Hotel. 'The arches striding o'er the new born stream, The village glittering in the noontide beam.'

His words were preserved and can be seen to this day.

Page 15

In Taymouth Castle Square, a fair was held each July – The Fair of the Holy Women. It was initiated by the Holy Sisters from the nearby nunnery on the Isle of Loch Tay. Once a year they would come out of their seclusion to market goods in aid of the poor. Tradition has it that The Sisters were later banished for 'scandalous behavior'.

The Campbells of Glenorchy subsequently used the convent as their castle. But in time, the infamous General Monk, sent by Cromwell to crush the Highland rebels, took possession of it.

On Drummond Hill there's a projecting crag, with a full view of Loch Tay. Known as the Black Rock, it is associated with the ancient defence system of the area. Its Gaelic name is 'Cragan an Eighich' – the 'Rock of Shouting'.

From its vantage point the human voice carries great distances. Lookouts placed here would shout warnings of an approaching enemy. Linked 'Rocks of Shouting' would often provide a line of communication for early civilisations.

At the eastern end of Drummond Hill there are remains of an ancient fort. Called Dun Mac Tual, it was one of a chain of forts running westwards through Glenlyon, each within sight of the next. It is thought, like the Rocks of Shouting, they were signal points where beacon fires would warn of danger.

A farm near the fort was called Achleys, meaning 'The Field of The Signal Fire'.

At Croft Moraig – which means The Field of Mary, there are concentric circles of large granite standing stones from pagan times. Outside of the stone circles lies a long slab with a number of cup hollows. This was possibly the altar stone of this pre-historic place of worship.

It is said that Robert Burns, during his visit to Breadalbane, in kindred spirit to these early worshippers, said his prayers here.

John Ruskin, the famous writer and art critic, during several visits to Scotland, remarked that fields of Scottish sheaves are as golden as 'the corn of Heaven'. He also described the deep, silent pools of the Tay as the 'pools of pausing'.

Page 16

High on a summit above Aberfeldy stood the prehistoric fort of Dun. It was one of the old chain of 'beacon forts'. A small loch, almost hidden in a hollow nearby, supplied the needs of its occupants. Ancient tradition has it that there is treasure concealed in the fort's foundations. It will be found one day by a lady with flowing red hair.

In the early 16th century, by a stream east of Aberfeldy, stood the smithy of Andrea Ferrara. Born in Italy, it's thought he was brought to Scotland by King James for his knowledge of the high-quality sword blades being made in Toledo.

From iron quarried from the surrounding hills he made his famous claymores. They became so renowned that blades of the highest quality became known as 'True Andrea Ferraras'. Even when used with the greatest force, they would scarcely ever break.

In Ossian's epic poem, it was said that Fingal's claymore was 'a sword which gives no second wound'.

General Wade's highland roads were constructed in Scotland to assist military control after the Jacobite rebellion in 1715. One ran from Crieff, past Aberfeldy to Dalnacardoch. They had a series of fortified garrisons whose soldiers helped quell the later risings under Bonnie Prince Charlie. In a way, they were an extension of the lowland roads built by the Romans to suppress the population there.

Page 17

Near the lonely tarn of Loch Hoil is a mound of grey stones. It has the name of 'Carn na mna uile' – The Cairn of The Wicked Woman. Legend says the last witch in the region was put to death here. It used to be that people who passed the cairn would throw stones to add to the mound.

Near Taybridge, the Black Watch – Am Freiceadan Dhubh, were mustered for the first time. A monument to commemorate the regiment's bravery was erected, crowned by the figure of a Highlander in uniform, right hand reaching for his sword. When the regiment was sent to Flanders in 1743, they became known as the 'Soldats Ecossais'.

Page 19

North-west of Aberfeldy, near to the village of Weem, General Wade's bridge spans the Tay. Constructed in 1733 to a design by William Adam, it was considered an 'architectural wonder'. The wonder disappeared when Sir John Cope, commander-in-chief in Scotland at the time of the '45 Jacobite rebellion, crossed over with troops and artillery, marching north to 'nip the rebellion in the bud'. (He later suffered an inglorious defeat at the Battle of Prestonpans, Bonnie Prince Charlie's first significant battle.)

In the wake of the Pretender's last battle - at Culloden, the Duke of Cumberland sent a detachment of troops to the bridge to trap and cut down any returning Jacobite survivors.

The village of Weem has also been known as Balclachan, derived from Gaelic – 'the town of the stones'. This leads some to think a Druidic circle once stood here, giving a religious significance to the site.
The name Weem itself comes from the Gaelic word 'uamh', meaning cave. About halfway up Weem Rock, there's an overhang called Craig-an-Chaipel – the Chapel Rock. Underneath there is a narrow cave.

A legend tells the strange story of two sisters searching for a stray calf. They followed the sound of its lowing to the cave in the rock. The bible one sister carried seemed to act as a charm to stop her from entering the cave. The other went fearlessly in and disappeared. Sometime later her mutilated body was found floating in Loch Ghlassie, in a weird phosphorescent light.

An old Gaelic song has the surviving girl asking when her little sister will come home. The strange reply tells of seven iron gates shielded by a sentry in a scarlet cloak, with a message that she cannot return until the Day of Judgement.

One can imagine the ghostly voice of the stricken sister saying they should look in Loch Ghlassie.

Castle Menzies, known earlier as Weem Castle, is thought to have been built in 1061. It was set on fire and partly destroyed in 1503, then later restored.

Castle Menzies' monument room contains many historical artefacts, including a set of bagpipes played at the Battle of Bannockburn. Unlike modern bagpipes there is only one drone. In consequence, to some ears, the tune can be heard more clearly.

Mary Queen of Scots was fond of hunting and took part in some of the great hunts at Castle Menzies. The 'Red and White Book of Menzies' mentions valuable relics from the times she stayed there. These include the famous 'Queen Mary's Cabinet'.

The Queen used to take walks in the old, tree- lined avenues and one of the sycamores was named after her.

Page 20

The House of Ballechin was traditionally owned by the Stewarts in a line dating back to Hector, a son of James 11. An old rhyme tells the legend of Sir James The Rose, an heir to the estate, who killed a Knight's squire.

Sir James fled to seek help from his lover. She hid him in a field of bracken where, exhausted from his escape, he fell asleep.

However, when his pursuers questioned the girl, she betrayed him and the avenging Knights fell upon Sir James in his bracken refuge. They killed him, took out his heart and mounted it on a spear. Then they showed it to his mortally-distressed sweetheart.

The old rhyme describes Sir James as the heir of 'Buleighen', which seems to connect the story to Ballechin. However, there seems to be another connection to the area of Loch Lagan.

The story lives on in modern times. Steeleye Span recorded a version as a song on their album, Rocket Cottage.

Ballechin House was once known as 'the most haunted house in Scotland'. Apparitions of ghostly nuns, a lady in a silk dress, and a dog were reported. Unexplained noises of knocking, clanging, quarrelling, and limping footsteps were heard. There were stories of something being dragged across the floor and the sound of a priest holding a service.

Page 21

The village of Logierait's ancient Gaelic name was Bal-na-Maoir, the town of the officials of justice. Once it was a place of great importance. Behind the township was a courthouse where feudal justice was administered. Criminals were summarily tried in a hall, situated conveniently close to the Gallow Hill.

When the Wolf of Badenoch controlled the district, little mercy was ever shown. Tradition recalls the execution of Allan McCrory, the legendary Chief of Clanranald, and the imprisonment of Rob Roy, probably for thieving cattle, who escaped before his trial was held.

Following the Battle of Prestonpans, 600 prisoners taken by the Jacobites were held in Logierait prison. There is no record of their fate.

Historian, James Irvine Robertson, tells the story of how a cattle thief, his head in the noose, was accosted by an old woman. She had lost her cow and asked the unfortunate rogue if, since he was so high up, he would have a look around for it.

There is another story of a shepherd, who, found guilty of stealing sheep, had his collie dog lynched beside him – as an accomplice.

High on the moors between Strathtummel and Strathtay, there's a group of Druidic 'Stones of Worship'. Part of their mysterious rites was to parade from East to West round the standing stones when entreating a blessing for their friends, or from West to East to put a curse on their enemies.

At Dunfallandy, there's a large sculptured stone of a kind peculiar to the East of Scotland. Called the 'Priest's Stone', it has on one side an Iona Cross with beautiful Celtic patterns. The other has a border of fish-tailed snakes, some figures, a crescent, and ancient mysterious, unexplained symbols.

Page 22

The trembling leaves of the aspens of Killiecrankie may have inspired its name, which means 'the shivering of the woods'. The Garry, one of the River Tay's tributaries flows through the Pass then joins the River Tummel to meet the Tay near Ballinluig.

The Battle of Killiecrankie, an important encounter of the first Jacobite rebellion, was fought in 1689. King James had invaded Ireland to reclaim his throne from William of Orange. In the King's support, James Graham, Viscount Dundee, raised his Standard in sight of the Tay on Dundee's Law Hill.

A government army was sent under Major-General Mackay to crush Graham's force. They met at the Pass of Killiecrankie, where, in less than thirty minutes, the Jacobites defeated an army twice their size.

In the last stages of the battle, 'Bonnie Dundee' was killed leading a cavalry charge.

The rebellion ended when King James was defeated at the Battle of the Boyne.

Page 23

The Mount of Blood is a translation of Dunfallandy. The site of a tragedy from an old ballad is marked by 'The Bloody Stone'. The legend is of an ill-fated courtship when the Laird of Tummelside plotted to win the heart of a Dunfallandy heiress. The tragic consequence led to the bloody murder of a rival, with the assassin lying in wait behind the huge stone.

Page 24

In 1808, the Duke of Atholl built the old bridge at Dunkeld, with its majestic seven arches. In some seasons, at noon on a clear still day, the arches can form perfect circles with their river shadows.

The Duke of Atholl was also famed for a peculiar act of forestry. He clothed the once bare slopes of Craig-y-Barns and Craig Vinean by firing seeds of pine, spruce and larch from a cannon. The seeds fell into cracks and ledges. In time they bloomed into the beautiful woodlands that grace the crags today.

Page 26

The Roman Fort at Inchtuthill, built during the reign of Septimus Severus, is situated between Caputh and Meikleour. Covering around 50 acres, it was built after the famous battle of Mons Graupius, as a major part of the Gaskhill Ridge line of 'Glenblocker Forts'. They were built to prevent Highlander incursions into Roman controlled territories. Probably the headquarters of the 20th Legion, it was never completed due to the forced withdrawal of Roman legions to defend their Empire in other parts of Europe.

Part of the fort's defences were encircling spikes of tree branches. These were called 'cervuli' from the latin 'cervus' – the antlers of deer.

Relics of pottery have been found at the site. Some were contemporaneous with those found in the ruins of Pompeii.

There are differing stories as to the location of the fabled Viking incursion which led to the humble thistle becoming Scotland's national emblem. One such locality was Stanley where a river crossing was named the 'Thistle Brig'.

The tale goes that as the Norsemen were advancing to attack a Scottish encampment, a bare footed soldier trod on a thistle. His yell of pain alerted the Scots, leading to a rout of the Vikings and the birth of the thistle legend.